Campfire Stories

Adaptation by Jamie White

Based on TV series teleplays

written by Bruce Akiyama and Ken Scarborough

Based on characters created by Susan Meddaugh

HOUGHTON MIFFLIN HARCOURT
Boston · New York · 2013

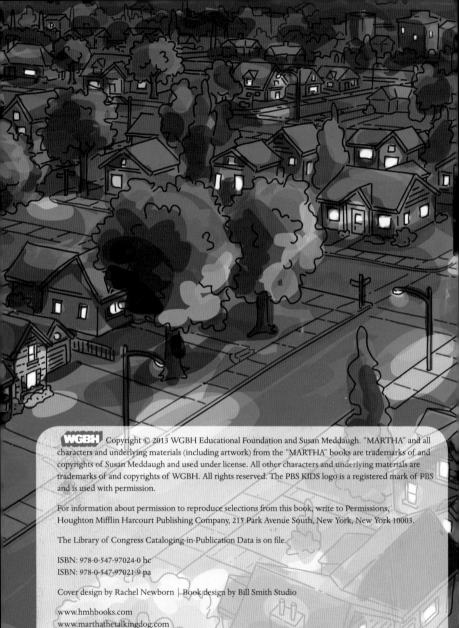

For information about permission to reproduce selections from this book, write to Permissions, Houghton Mifflin Harcourt Publishing Company, 215 Park Avenue South, New York, New York 10003.

The Library of Congress Cataloging-in-Publication Data is on file.

ISBN: 978-0-547-97024-0 hc
ISBN: 978-0-547-97021-9 pa

Cover design by Rachel Newborn | Book design by Bill Smith Studio

www.hmhbooks.com
www.marthathetalkingdog.com

Manufactured in China
SCP 10 9 8 7 6 5 4 3 2 1
4500394162 | 4500394161 (pb)

MARTHA SAYS "BEWARE"

Beware, Martha fans! For the next eighty-nine pages, I will be taking you on a journey into the realm of the improbable, the unpredictable, and the unforeseen . . .

Things that are unforeseen are things that you didn't know would happen.

OOGLEY BOOGLEY!

See? I bet you didn't know you were going to read the words "Oogley boogley"! It was totally unforeseen. Know what else was unforeseen? A talking dog.

Ever since Helen fed me her alphabet soup, I've been able to speak. And speak and speak . . . No one's sure how or why, but the letters in the soup traveled up to my brain instead of down to my stomach.

Steak is at the base of my food pyramid, along with alphabet soup. Above that is just meat in general.

Now as long as I eat my daily bowl of alphabet soup, I can talk. To my family—Helen, baby Jake, Mom, Dad, and Skits, who only speaks Dog. To Helen's friends—T.D., Truman, and Alice. To anyone who'll listen.

Sometimes my family wishes I didn't talk quite so much. But my speaking comes in handy. Like the time I called 911 to stop a burglar. Or when I share spooky stories while we're camping.

Want to hear some for yourself?

Read on . . . if you dare!

SLUMBER PARTY OF THE WEIRD

Sleeping on the ground, cooking with sticks, frightening each other with scary stories . . . humans sure have weird ways of having fun.

I don't get camping. Who wants to sleep outside when there are comfy chairs in the house? What am I, a squirrel? I also don't understand why Helen calls our tent a pup tent when it could easily fit three full-grown Great Danes.

And yet, one summer night, there I was—camping out in the backyard with Helen, Skits, T.D., Alice, and Truman. It was late and we were running out of ways to entertain ourselves. We'd been making shadow puppets for more than an hour.

It was T.D.'s turn. First he made a bird shadow. Then he raised two fingers into the air to make a bunny.

I think we're done here, I thought, pressing the flashlight's Off button.

"Hoppity-hop. Hey! Where'd that bunny go?" he said.

"Now what?" said Alice.

"How about a dog?" Helen suggested.

"I did a dog," Alice replied. "I did a whole pack of dogs. And an ostrich and a crab . . ."

T.D. sighed. "It's official. We've done every hand shadow known to kid."

"So what do we do?" asked Alice.

Helen shrugged. "I don't know. We ate all the s'mores."

"The chocolate-free ones were delicious," I said, licking the last of the marshmallow off my nose.

"If we play go fish one more time," said Truman, "I'm going to be seasick."

Next to us, Skits snored. But I wasn't tired yet. "There has to be *something* we can do," I said.

"I know!" said T.D. "We could make up science fiction stories!"

"Great," said Alice in a bored voice. "I had this hypothesis, and my experiment proved I was correct. The end. Yawn!"

"Well, it might help make us sleepy," I said.

"Science fiction stories aren't about science," said T.D. "I mean, they are, sort of. But mostly they're made-up stories that take place in space or the future. A lot of times they have aliens or spaceships."

Truman's eyes grew wide. "A-a-aliens? We might give ourselves nightmares."

"Cool!" said Alice and T.D. together.

"Does anyone here know a good science fiction story?" T.D. asked.

"I've got one," I said.

"Martha?" asked Helen, surprised. "You do?"

"Yes," I said. "It's a mystery, full of strange and, uh, mysterious things. It's unpredictable. No one can guess what might happen!"

Everybody but Truman seemed interested. He scrunched down into his sleeping bag. "I'm hiding in here," he said, "just in case it gets scary."

"Okay," I said. "My story starts on the hottest day of July. T.D. was selling lemonade . . ."

THE VISITORS
Martha's Story

"Lemonade! Get your lemonade!" T.D. called.

He'd set up a stand in front of his house and was expecting lots of customers. Human customers. But then . . .

"I'll take one," came a robotic voice.

T.D. looked up to see two unusual tourists wearing Hawaiian shirts.

"Whoa," said T.D.

The male alien grabbed a cup of lemonade. He poured it into his ear. *Glug, glug, glug!*

"Ahhh. Wow!" he said. "Tastes great!"

"You aren't from around here, are you?" asked T.D.

"Um, no," the alien said. "We're here to gather data about your town."

T.D. was confused. "Data?" he asked.

"Data," said the alien, "is information, like facts. When you gather data, you find out about something. You collect facts."

"So when you say you want to gather data about our town, you mean you just want to know all about it?" asked T.D.

"Yes," the alien replied.

T.D. smiled wide. "Well, you've come to the right guy!"

T.D. showed the visitors all around Wagstaff City. They took pictures of everything they saw.

First T.D. took them to the bowling alley. It turns out that aliens aren't very good bowlers. Instead of letting go of the ball, Mr. Alien held on tight.

"Aagh!" he cried as the ball dragged him down the lane. Luckily, he reappeared in the ball return.

Next they went to the mini-golf course. But the aliens spent the whole time bowing to a giant purple dinosaur at the fifth hole.

Then they ate frozen yogurt in the park. (T.D. was only a little embarrassed when the aliens ate it with their ears.)

But hey, they did make a cool spaceship out of sand at the beach. And back at T.D.'s house, they earned the top score of T.D.'s Alien Invasion video game.

After giving the aliens a complete tour of town, T.D. rang our doorbell. *Ding-dong!*

Helen opened the door. Her jaw dropped.

"These are the Willards," said T.D., introducing his new friends. "Martin and Sylvia. They're from the planet Venus. Okay if they look around?"

"Um . . ." said Helen.

Without waiting for a reply, the aliens marched past her and into our living room. Sylvia began inspecting it while Martin took pictures. *Click! Click!*

I watched them look around. "What on earth is happening?" I wondered aloud.

"They're gathering data," T.D. explained.

But when they began measuring the windows, I smelled trouble. "Something weird is going on here," I said.

The aliens moved on to the kitchen. Sylvia turned the sink's faucet on and off, on and off. Martin opened our stove. He even peeked into our cupboards.

"There's something peculiar about those two aliens," I whispered to Helen and T.D. "I get the feeling they aren't gathering data. I think . . . they're *moving in!*"

A BONE-HEADED ENDING

Things got even stranger in the backyard. From a safe distance away, Helen, T.D., and I watched Martin aim some kind of remote control at the ground. He pressed a button. In an instant, an enormous alien flower shot up and bloomed. It was the biggest flower I'd ever seen.

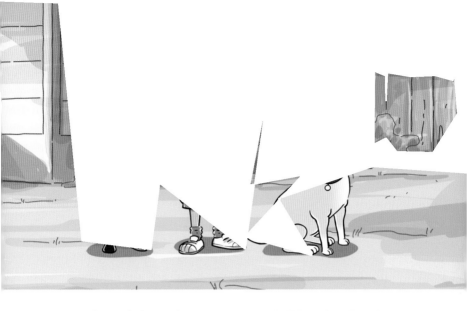

"What did I tell you?" I said. "Look, they're already planting a garden!"

"Well, I guess it wouldn't hurt to ask what they're doing," said Helen.

"You go ahead," said T.D., taking a step back toward the house.

"They're your friends!" Helen protested.

But he looked scared. "I'm not going to do it. Martha, you go."

I sighed. Why is it always up to the dog?

25

Trying to appear casual, I strolled over to the aliens, who were busy tending their big weird plant.

The aliens glared at me. They staggered toward me like zombies . . .

"Holy hamburgers!" I shouted, running back to Helen and T.D.

Helen tried to stay calm. "Okay, listen," she said to them. "Let's discuss this, shall we?"

But the aliens didn't reply. Instead they stepped closer . . . and closer . . .

"Yikes!" I exclaimed. "Somebody, help!"

Just then, we heard a familiar *woof woof!*

Skits poked his head out the back door.

"Skits!" Helen cried.

"Aha!" I said to the aliens. "Now the tables have turned. The hunter becomes the hunted. I'm warning you—this dog is *mean.*"

Skits ran circles around Martin and Sylvia, giving them a sniff.

"Yeah, that's right. Skits is mean," I went on, "and he's—"

Oh no, I thought as Skits rolled onto his back for a belly rub. *How embarrassing.*

"Um, okay," I said. "He's just putting on an act now to fool you. Ha ha! But you watch, he's going to—"

Woof, woof!

Skits ran to the side of the yard and began to dig.

"He's going to dig up a bone to give you," I muttered. "Great."

"Oh well," said T.D. "You might as well turn us into aliens or whatever." He looked at me and Helen. "Sorry about this, guys."

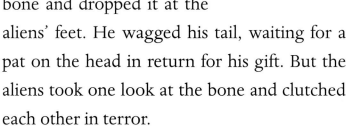

Skits dug up the
bone and dropped it at the
aliens' feet. He wagged his tail, waiting for a
pat on the head in return for his gift. But the
aliens took one look at the bone and clutched
each other in terror.

"AAAAAHHHHHH!" they shrieked, running
away.

"Huh? What was that
about?" Helen asked
as we watched them
disappear down the
street.

Moments later, back on board their space-ship, the aliens reported on the day to their king.

"We've concluded that we can't invade, Your Highness," said Martin. "Those earth people are scary! We just witnessed the meanest thing we've ever seen. You would never be safe there, Your Highness! We must leave! Quickly!"

And after hearing their story, the king couldn't agree more.

The spaceship shot out of sight, never to be seen again.

NIGHTMARE IN THE TREE

"Now, that was science fiction!" said T.D. "I give it four stars."

Truman poked his head out of his sleeping bag. "That wasn't too scary."

In the darkness, Alice flinched. "But *that* is!"
she said.

"What?" Helen whispered.

"That thing flying outside our tent!" Alice said, pointing at a shadow on the tent wall.

We screamed.

"What *is* that?" asked Helen.

"Whatever it is, it's going to give me nightmares," Truman squeaked.

"What's a nightmare?" I asked.

"A nightmare is a bad dream," Alice explained.

"Oh, like when I dreamt the pet shop gave me a ton of free dog food but forgot to include the can opener?" I asked.

"Uh, sure," said Alice. She cautiously unzipped the tent to see the creature more closely. We all peeked out as she shined her flashlight on it. "Look!" she said. "Over there!"

We looked up. Somebody—or some*thing*—
in a long coat hovered in the tree! We
couldn't see its face, only its sleeves flapping in
the breeze.

"It's a GHOST!" shouted Truman.

"AHHHHHHHHHHHHHHHHHH!" we all screamed.

Finally, Helen stopped. "Hey!" she said. "That's not a ghost. It's just my rain slicker! I left it on the gate and the wind must have blown it up there."

"Oh," I said, feeling silly. "I knew that."

"Okay," said T.D. "My turn to tell a story."
He took out his pen and yellow pad. "I have a
good one to share. It starts with Martha."

And then T.D. told the scariest story I had
ever heard . . .

MEET THE FELINES
T.D.'s Story

One day, Martha was sitting in her yard when she got an invitation. Helen asked her to take a walk with her and her dad.

"We're off to visit our new neighbors, the Felines," she said. "They just moved in down the block."

Helen's dad

Helen

Martha

"We're going to stop by and say hi," said Dad. "Come with us!"

Martha joined them, even though something didn't seem quite right. All the way there, she kept saying to herself, "Feline . . . feline . . . feline." *Hmm,* she thought. *I feel like I've heard that name before. But where?*

They stopped at a cheery little house. Mr. and Mrs. Feline welcomed them inside. They seemed nice enough. So why did Martha still feel so strange?

While Mrs. Feline cooked in the kitchen, they talked to Mr. Feline in their living room.

"It's so nice to meet you," Mr. Feline said to them. "We just love Wagstaff Cit—"

Suddenly, he froze and stared hard at a bird hopping on the windowsill. *Now that's peculiar,* Martha thought.

"Um, you were saying?" said Dad.

Mr. Feline turned back to them. "What? Oh! Just that we love it here."

At that moment, Mrs. Feline came into the room. "Would you care to join us for lunch?" she asked.

"And how!" Martha blurted out. "Uh, speaking for the group, that is."

In the kitchen, they gathered to eat. Martha sniffed at the soup in her dog bowl. It didn't smell as good as her favorite—alphabet soup. But hey, Martha eats from the garbage, so she figured she couldn't complain.

"Mmm," said Dad. "Smells delicious. What is it?"

"It's an old family recipe," said Mrs. Feline.

"It's called . . ." said her husband, "MOUSE SOUP!"

"Ack," Martha said, her stomach turning.

Helen looked queasy too.

"Oh, er, yum," said Dad.

"I'll go get more spoons," said Mrs. Feline.

Martha looked around the room. *Yup,* she thought. *There is definitely something mysterious about the Feline family.*

In the living room, the Felines' baby crawled on the couch. He stopped to scratch the fabric. And . . . sharpen his claws? The baby leaped on the back of the couch to scowl at the bird on the windowsill.

Hiss! went the baby.

"We have to get out of here!" Martha said
to Helen and Dad.

"Why?" Dad asked.

"I just remembered what *feline* means!"

Everybody stared at Martha, waiting. But
she was too scared to speak.

"Yesssss?" asked Mr. and Mrs. Feline, narrowing their eyes at Martha. "What does *feline* mean?"

"A feline is a . . . a . . . " Martha stammered.

But before she could say the dreaded word, the Felines reached for their faces. They whipped off the masks they were wearing to reveal . . .

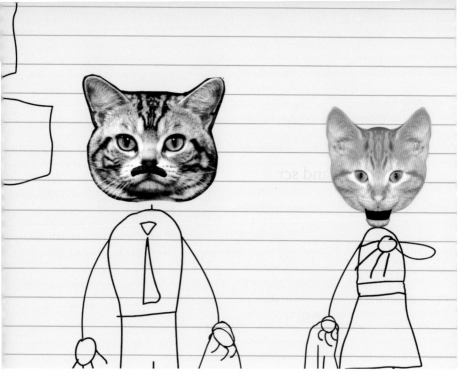

"CAT!" Martha shrieked.

The Felines weren't human at all. They were actually cat people from another planet!

"Meow," said Mrs. Feline.

"Meow," mewed Mr. Feline.

"Awww!" said Dad. "Cute."

"Cute?!" Martha shouted. "They're cats! RUN!"

Helen and Martha took off screaming.

"Oh, all right," Dad sighed. He threw his arms into the air and screamed too. "AHHHHHH!"

They fled from the Felines.

Meow! Meow! Hiss! The Felines were catching up. The other three had to think fast.

"This way!" Martha said, heading toward the lake. Helen and Dad caught up to her at the water's edge.

"The lake?" asked Helen.

"Cats hate water," Martha explained. "Quick! Dive in!"

Splash! They ran into the lake and paddled out until the Felines looked like tiny fur balls on the shore. Sure enough, the cats didn't dip a paw into the water.

"Drat," said Mr. Feline.

"Meow," went Mrs. Feline.

Finally, they gave up and left.

Martha, Helen, and Dad made it home safe and sound. Helen and Martha talked in the kitchen while Dad cooked lunch.

"Phew!" said Helen. "That was a close one!"

"I'll say," Martha agreed. "If those cat people had caught us, they'd probably turn us into cats too!"

Dad chuckled from where he stood at the counter. He was stirring something in a big bowl. "I'll bet you two are hungry after all that," he said.

"I'm starving. What have you got?" Martha asked, sniffing a familiar smell.

"Some delicious . . ." he said, turning around. "MOUSE SOUP!"

Dad's whiskers twitched menacingly.

"CAAAAAAT!" Helen and Martha cried. "AHHHHHHHHHHH!"

"Meow," said Dad.

SOMETHING WEIRD

"That's the end?" said Truman. "You're ending it with being cats?"

"Scary, right?" said T.D.

I scooted closer to Helen. "But . . . that couldn't really happen, could it?"

T.D. leaned toward me. "Maybe," he whispered.

"Don't frighten her," scolded Helen. "It's just science fiction, Martha. The *fiction* part means it's made up."

Alice sighed. "Why don't you tell us a story, Helen? It might take Martha's mind off the Felines."

"All right," Helen said. "My story is called 'The Telltale Artichoke Heart.' It begins one dark and stormy night at our house. Something weird was going on . . ."

THE TELLTALE ARTICHOKE HEART

Helen's Story

I was nervous. Very, very nervous. I was then and still am.

Outside my bedroom window, thunder rumbled and lightning cracked. But I heard something else, too. From somewhere within my house came a strange sound. A sound like a heart beating.

Thump. Thump. Thump.

The noise was so loud that it woke Martha. Her ears perked up and she shivered a little. I was scared too, but I was also curious about the sound, so I slipped out of bed and grabbed a candelabra to light our way. The candlelight quivered in the inky night as we crept toward the thumping. It sounded like it was coming from downstairs.

Martha and I held our breath to listen closely.

"Did you hear it, Martha?" I whispered. "That ominous sound in the darkness?"

The beating grew louder.

Thump. Thump. Thump.

"Does *ominous* mean you think something bad will happen?" she asked with a shaky voice.

"Right," I said.

"Well, then I heard it," she said. "It's ominous, all right."

We tiptoed downstairs. I was so frightened, I wondered if the sound was from my own heart, which felt like it was going to beat out of my chest.

THUMP. THUMP. THUMP.

"It's coming from the kitchen," Martha whispered.

We inched toward the kitchen's closed door. With a soft push, I swung it open. What we saw made us both gasp. A flash of lightning illuminated the dark outline of a boy. Somebody *was* in the kitchen!

I'd recognize that silhouette anywhere.

"T.D.!" I cried. "What are *you* doing here?"

T.D. looked nervous. "Um, er, nothing? I didn't hide anything, I swear!"

"Hide anything?" I said.

"Were *you* making that ominous noise?" Martha asked.

"What ominous noise?" he replied.

"That thumping," I said. "Listen . . . there it is again!"

THUMP. THUMP. THUMP.

Martha pawed at a tile of the kitchen floor. "Here!" she said. "The noise is coming from under here!"

T.D. threw up his hands. "Okay! I admit it! I hid it there! I couldn't stand to have it in our pantry and the noise was keeping me up all night, so I brought it over here."

He pulled up the tile, removing a tin can. It pulsed with each *thump.* Confused, I grabbed the can and read its label.

"Canned artichoke hearts?"

Just then, the lid popped open and—*boing!*—a smiling artichoke heart jumped out of the can. He landed on the lid with a giggle. T.D. screamed.

"Good evening and welcome to the show!" he said into a tiny microphone. "Just what is a walking, talking artichoke heart doing in your kitchen? Funny you should ask! So for my first impression I'm going to make like a watercolor and . . . *run!*"

The artichoke heart leaped onto the floor. In a flash, he scurried to the doggie door.

"Well, this is a first," said T.D. "I've run away from my vegetables before, but I've never had one run away from me. Go get it, Helen!"

"You brought it here!" I said.

But T.D. looked scared. "Martha, you go."

Martha rolled her eyes. "Not again," she said.

At the door, the artichoke heart turned back to us. "Don't forget," he said. "I'm here every night for dinner . . . *not!*" Then with a crazy laugh, he pushed open the door and ran across the yard.

"Now, *that* was unexpected," I said. "Who knew canned goods could be so creepy?"

"I did," said T.D. "Lima beans terrify me!"

We raced to the window to see the artichoke heart fleeing as fast as his little legs could carry him. He disappeared into the night and was never seen again.

But he's still out there somewhere, hiding in someone's kitchen, lurking in a cabinet.

Maybe even . . . *yours!*

S'MORE STORIES

Truman shuddered. "Artichoke hearts on the run!" he exclaimed. "Cats pretending to be humans! Aliens invading Wagstaff City! No more stories. How am I *ever* going to sleep tonight?"

"But that can't be the last story," Helen said. "Martha, could you tell us one more? Please?"

"That depends," I said. "Are there any more s'mores—hold-the-chocolate, extra marsh-mallows—coming?"

"Martha! You've already eaten an entire tray of them," said Alice.

"Yes," I said. "But that was a whole twenty minutes ago."

Helen sighed.

"Oh, all right," Alice said. "I'll tell a story. It's called 'Night of the Phantom Scarecrow.' It begins on a lonely park road just as darkness falls . . ."

NIGHT OF THE PHANTOM SCARECROW

Alice's Story

The dark, wooded road was eerily quiet. The only noise came from Helen and me tossing my volleyball back and forth. Martha was with us, and we were on our way home after a long day at the beach.

Suddenly, I saw something up ahead that made me stop in my tracks. "Look!" I said.

A few yards away, Helen's dad's car was parked at the side of the road. He was fixing a flat tire.

"Hi, Dad!" said Helen as we approached him. "Do you need some help?"

"Oh, I'll manage," he said. "But you three should get home quickly. Darkness is coming. The Phantom Scarecrow will be here soon."

Helen and I exchanged uneasy looks.

"Phantom?" Martha said, sounding worried. "What's a phantom?"

"A phantom is something that isn't really there," he said.

"Like a ghost?" asked Helen.

"Yes," said Helen's dad. "Or like the spare tire I thought I saw in here last week." He sighed. "Now go on, hurry home!"

He didn't need to tell us again. We left him behind and moved on. The sun had set, making the woods look spookier than ever.

"There's no such thing as a Phantom Scarecrow, is there?" Martha asked.

"No way," I said, "and if there was, this is what I'd do to it!" I tossed the volleyball into the air and—*whack!*—spiked it into a bush. Leaves scattered everywhere.

"Take that," I said, and nodded.

"Nice serve," Martha said.

"Thanks." Then I strode over to the bush to get my ball. But when I parted the branches to grab it, I saw something that made me freeze. I couldn't stop staring. I opened my mouth to scream, but no sound came out. Martha and Helen ran over, and they saw too. Just behind the volleyball was a pair of legs . . . with no feet!

We all looked up and gasped. The body of
a scarecrow hovered in midair. And it was
missing more than feet. It was headless, too!

"Agghh!" we shrieked. "The Phantom!"

I dropped the ball. As it started to bounce
down the road, the Phantom quickly snatched
it up. It placed the ball on its shoulders where
its head should be.

"Heh, heh, heh!" it cackled, clapping its straw hands.

Then it lunged toward us. Martha squeezed her eyes shut, not daring to look. I grabbed Helen and held on tight. We all screamed again.

But instead of grabbing us in its grassy grip, the Phantom brushed quickly past. With a jump, it waved goodbye and skipped down the road, happy to finally have a head, even if it was just my volleyball.

We ran home as fast as we could and didn't look back.

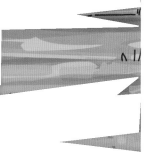

We never saw the Phantom Scarecrow again. But it's still out there. They say it now haunts the local beaches. Mostly during volleyball season.

MARTHA SAYS "SLEEP TIGHT"

"That's it," said Helen. "No more trips to the beach for us!"

"Aw, come on," said T.D. "Do you really expect a volleyball to be scary?"

"You've clearly never tripped over one in a dark room before," Alice muttered.

"We'd better go to sleep now," said Truman. "I've heard enough spooky stories to last me a lifetime."

The tent was finally quiet as I snuggled in among everyone's sleeping bags. All we could hear were crickets chirping and Skits snoring. But then out of the darkness came a loud *GROWL!*

The kids screamed.

"MONSTER!" yelled Truman.

"Um," I said. "I think that was my stomach."

Helen laughed. "Oh, Martha!"

That night, we all had a little trouble falling asleep. But I knew those stories weren't true. At least, I don't think they're true. *They can't be true, right!?*

If only someone could explain how Alice's volleyball got into our tent while we were were sleeping . . .

THE END?

How many words do you remember from the story?

data: information, like facts

enormous: really, really big

feline: cat

nightmare: bad dream

ominous: threatening, suggesting that something bad will happen soon

phantom: something that isn't really there

science fiction: made-up stories that take place in space or the future

silhouette: outline of a dark shape against a bright light

unforeseen: not predicted ahead of time

Campfire Story Starters

Want to tell your own science fiction story? Martha has lent a paw to help you get started. Using words from the glossary, try finishing the tales below!

The Invisible Dog
A mad scientist has perfected disappearing ink. But—uh-oh!—a drop has landed in Martha's water dish and she just drank it . . .

The Mysterious Moonseeds
T.D. visits a farmer's market on the moon. After tasting some delicious grapes, he wants to grow his own. The space farmer warns, "If you plant them on earth, no one knows what might happen." But T.D. plants one of the mysterious seeds in his backyard anyway . . .

The Haunted Pup Tent
While Martha and the kids are sleeping, Alice's volleyball mysteriously ends up in their tent. How did it get there?

Silly Silhouettes

a.

b.

c.

Do you recognize these silhouettes? (Answers below.)

You and your friends can use your silhouettes to put on a shadow play. Hang a white sheet from a doorway or ceiling in a darkened room. Set up chairs in front of the sheet for your audience. Then place a bright, unshaded lamp behind the sheet. Stand on the lit side of the sheet and act out your favorite scene from this book!